CIP Data is available.

Published in the United States 2000 by Dutton Children's Books,
a division of Penguin Putnam Books for Young Readers
345 Hudson Street, New York, New York 10014
http://www.penguinputnam.com/yreaders/index.htm

Originally published in Great Britain 1999 by Andersen Press Ltd., London
Typography by Richard Amari
Printed in Italy First American Edition
ISBN 0-525-46386-0
2 4 6 8 10 9 7 5 3 1

# Kiss It Better

by **Hiawyn Oram**

illustrated by **Frédéric Joos**

DUTTON CHILDREN'S BOOKS · NEW YORK

Little Bear was playing on the floor…

and hit her head on the table.

"Oh, dear," said Big Bear. "I'll kiss it better."

Little Bear was standing on a stool, reaching for the highest shelf…

when she slipped and bumped her paw.

"Oh, dear," said Big Bear. "I'll kiss it better."

Little Bear was playing on the playground.

Her best friend didn't want to be her best friend anymore,

and her second-best friend didn't want
to be her second-best friend anymore.

"Not a good day," sighed Little Bear that night.

"Oh, dear," said Big Bear. "I'll kiss it better."

And the next day, things did seem better. Little Bear made a new best friend…

and decided that her old best friend could be her new second-best friend.

But when she got home, she found Big Bear slumped on the sofa, reading a letter.

"Is it bad news?" whispered Little Bear.
"Yes, it's bad," sighed Big Bear.
"Really bad?" said Little Bear.
"Really bad," said Big Bear.

"Oh, dear," said Little Bear. "I'll kiss it better."
So Little Bear kissed Big Bear's tummy and Big Bear's nose...

from Big Bear's top

to Big Bear's toes...

and Big Bear
where it tickled...

and Big Bear
where it didn't...

and Big Bear all over, until Big Bear smiled and Big Bear laughed and Big Bear cried, "Stop, Little Bear, stop!"

"Are you sure?" said Little Bear. "Does it feel all better now?"

"Noooo..." said Big Bear, "but it doesn't feel half so bad!"

"Don't worry—that's only because I forgot something," said Little Bear, jumping up and running out of the room.

"I forgot THESE!"